To Sheila Perry,
who first introduced me to
the glories of Venice

ATHENEUM BOOKS FOR YOUNG READERS
An imprint of Simon & Schuster Children's Publishing Division
1230 Avenue of the Americas, New York, New York 10020
Text and illustrations copyright © 2010 by Ian Falconer
Additional photographs copyright © 2010 by Rick Guidotti
All rights reserved, including the right of reproduction in whole
or in part in any form.
ATHENEUM BOOKS FOR YOUNG READERS is a registered trademark
of Simon & Schuster, Inc.
For information about special discounts for bulk purchases,
please contact Simon & Schuster Special Sales at
1-866-506-1949 or business@simonandschuster.com.
The Simon & Schuster Speakers Bureau can bring authors to
your live event. For more information or to book an event,
contact the Simon & Schuster Speakers Bureau at
1-866-248-3049 or visit our website at www.simonspeakers.com.
Book design by Ann Bobco
The text for this book is set in Centaur.
The illustrations for this book are rendered in charcoal and gouache
on paper, combined with photographs digitally altered
in Photoshop.
Special thanks to Ann Bobco and Paul Colin. Ann has been the
art director and book designer since the first Olivia book, and Paul
likes pigs. Without their skills, this book would not have been
possible. Many, many thanks.
Manufactured in China
0710 KWO
First Edition
10 9 8 7 6 5 4 3 2 1
Library of Congress Cataloging-in-Publication Data
Falconer, Ian, 1959–
Olivia goes to Venice / written and illustrated by
Ian Falconer. —1st ed.
p. cm.
Summary: On a family vacation in Venice, Olivia indulges in
gelato, rides in a gondola, and finds the perfect souvenir.
ISBN 978-1-4169-9674-3 (hardcover)
[1. Pigs—Fiction. 2. Vacations—Fiction. 3. Venice (Italy)—Fiction.
4. Italy—Fiction.] I. Title.
PZ7.F1865Oln 2010
[E]—dc22   2010009589

OLIVIA

goes to

Venice

written and illustrated by   Ian Falconer

ATHENEUM BOOKS FOR YOUNG READERS

New York   London   Toronto   Sydney

It was time for spring vacation. Olivia decided that she and her family ought to spend a few days in Venice. There was a lot of packing to be done.

"Olivia, you won't be needing your snorkel," said her mother, "or your flippers."

"Mother, apparently the city is often under water and—"

"Or your water skis."

As they went through the airport, Olivia was searched
for weapons. She was very pleased.

On the plane Olivia asked her mother about the food in Venice.

"Don't worry, sweetheart, you can get pizza and ice cream everywhere."

"EVERYWHERE?!"

Olivia was relieved.

They arrived very late at their hotel. Olivia was so sleepy,
she didn't even notice the view from her window.

Early the next morning
they set forth.
They crossed a pretty
little bridge.
And then another.
And then another.

"Wait!"
cried Olivia.

"We've been crossing the same canal!
I think we're lost. And my blood sugar
is getting low."

"We'll get some ice cream,"
promised her mother.

"It's called gelato,"
replied Olivia.

They all decided to have gelato.

Crossing a big bridge, Olivia saw the Grand Canal for the first time, lined with its glittering many-colored palazzos.

Olivia said to her mother with an edge of hysteria in her voice, "Oh, please— OH, PLEASE, MOTHER— can't we live in a palazzo on the Grand Canal?"

It was a life-changing experience for Olivia. She needed another gelato.

Or maybe two . . .

. . . or three.

When she was refreshed, they wandered on.

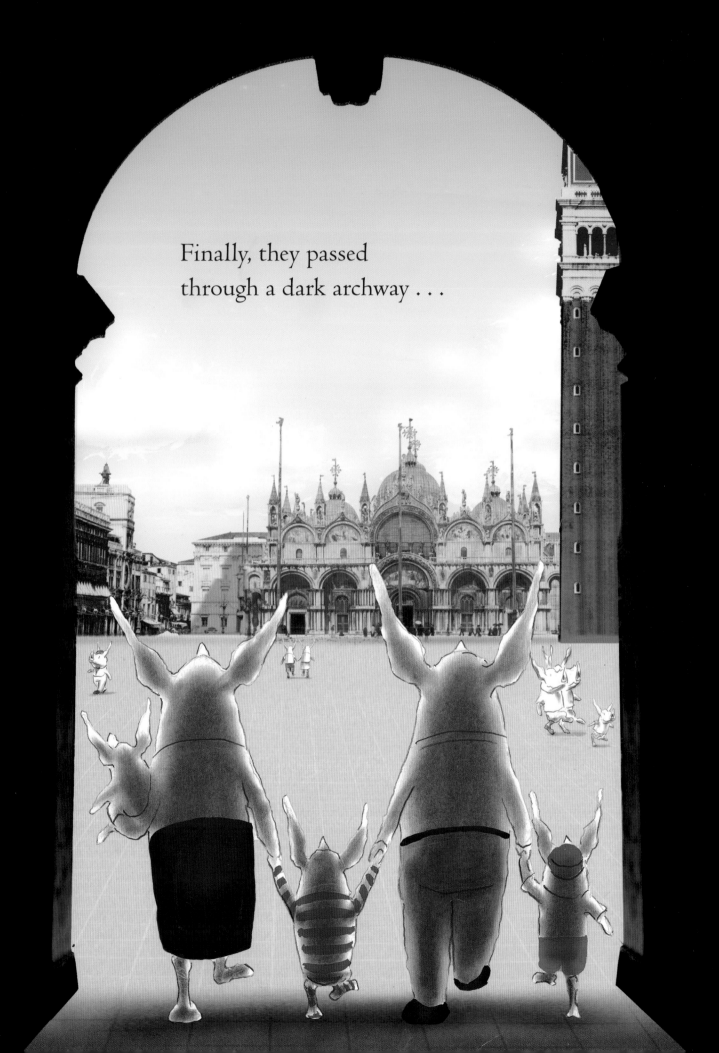

Finally, they passed
through a dark archway . . .

. . . and into the Piazza San Marco.
Olivia was overcome by its beauty. "Mother,
I think I could use another—"

Her mother sighed. "I think we all could."

Olivia wanted to buy corn
to feed the pigeons.

She held out the corn, but
couldn't find many pigeons.

But they soon found her.

After that exhausting encounter
Olivia required another gelato.

GONDOLA!
GONDOLA!

The next day Olivia begged her parents, "Oh, Mommy, Daddy—PLEASE can we take a gondola ride?"

Olivia negotiated the price. The gondolier waved them aboard with a gallant *"Prego."*

Olivia found it very restful.
The gondolier did not.

They came out onto the Grand Canal and passed under the magnificent Rialto Bridge.

Eventually they emerged
out from under the
Bridge of Sighs.

Olivia sighed.

By now, Olivia was
completely entranced.
"I must have something
to remember Venice by.
I must find the perfect
souvenir.

"How about a chandelier?"

"Olivia, that's bigger than your
room!" said her mother.

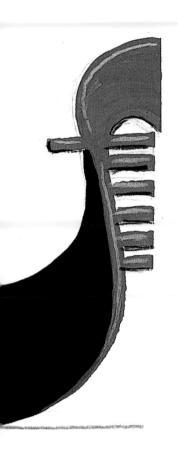

"What about a gondola?"

"Sweetheart, try to find something you can carry."

Lace?

Very pretty, but not really very Olivia.

A mask?

No, thought Olivia, *I'll only wear it once.*

Perfume?

Olivia doesn't really like perfume.

Besides, she's planning her own line.

On their last day in Venice, Olivia and her family went back
to San Marco.

The basilica was all peach and
gold in the late afternoon light.
Mother and Father were finishing
their coffee. Olivia and Ian were
playing by the bell tower.

"I found it!" cried Olivia. "The perfect souvenir!"
"What is that?" asked her mother.
"One of the actual Stones of Venice," said Olivia.
"From the bell tower."

"OLIVIA!" said her mother.
"If everyone took a piece of Venice
with them, the city would fall down.
Now leave that with the waiter.
We've got to get to the airport."

Olivia turned to take one last look at Venice.

"Look, they're waving us good-bye. . . .

I'll always remember Venice,
Mommy. Do you think
Venice will remember me?"

"Probably."

As soon as she got on the plane, Olivia fell fast asleep . . .

On the monument:

OLIVIA
ADMMX

On the sign:

MONUMENTO
OLIVIA
←

. . . and dreamed.